William Smith Morris

An Unconditional Surrender

A Comedy in Three Acts

William Smith Morris

An Unconditional Surrender
A Comedy in Three Acts

ISBN/EAN: 9783337054144

Printed in Europe, USA, Canada, Australia, Japan

Cover: Foto ©Andreas Hilbeck / pixelio.de

More available books at **www.hansebooks.com**

AN

Unconditional Surrender

A Comedy in Three Acts

BY

WILLIAM SMITH MORRIS, M. D.

Philadelphia
The Penn Publishing Company
1892

DRAMATIS PERSONÆ

Mr. Lennox Colfax, *a popular novelist from New York.*

Mr. Harrison Pennington, *a Philadelphia broker.*

Mr. Ward Van Artsdalen, *a New York broker.*

Miss Belle Walling, *a Baltimore belle.*

Miss Dolly Mayfair, *a Philadelphia belle.*

Miss May McCollum, *a New York belle.*

Eddie, *the colored bell boy.*

Chloe, *Eddie's sweetheart (appearing only en tableau.)*

Colonel Lee, *who does not appear at all.*

Time Required, 2½ Hours.

ARGUMENT

Three "Society Belles"—Miss Walling, of Baltimore ; Miss Mayfair, of Philadelphia ; and Miss McCollum, of New York—are boarding at the Hotel Elberon, at Elberon, on the Jersey coast. In the First Act Belle and her two friends engage in a lively dialogue, in which, among other things, the latest novel of Lennox Colfax, a popular novelist, who is also stopping at the hotel, is discussed. In the midst of the talk he appears and is compelled to endure their joint assault upon his story, for creating such namby-pamby heroines.

A literary partnership is suggested—or a course in love—to teach him, more correctly, of the divine passion, as well as of women. After his exit, Mr. Harrison Pennington, a Philadelphia broker, appears, vowing vengeance on his quondam chum, Ward Van Artsdalen, a New York broker, for calling him a "liar." A duel is imminent. The girls—Dolly and May—take sides with the doughty representatives of their respective cities. Belle and Mr. Colfax concoct a scheme to render the duel bloodless, and the combat becomes a ludicrous farce, the Act ending with an umbrella *denouement*, in which the two duelists find a balm for their injured feelings in a fetching love scene.

In the *Third Act* the course of true love is found to have run its proverbially crooked course. The lovers have quarreled and separated. Everything is topsy-turvey. Belle has learned to love the author while assisting in writing his new story, but he seems blind to her charms.

The brokers concoct a plan to flirt with each other's *ex-fiancees*, thinking that such a resort may bring their loves back to them. Eddie, the bell boy, defeats this scheme, by unwittingly changing the notes he has been commissioned to deliver.

The result is unexpected to the men, but lovely, nevertheless. Finally the author and Belle meet in the rustic pavilion for the purpose of completing the love story, upon which they have been engaged for three weeks. The love scene doesn't seem to suit. He suggests that they enact it—assuming the characters of the lovers. Result, unforeseen—from jest to earnest. He proposes to Belle, is accepted, and with an affecting tableau, in which Cupid is triumphant, the curtain descends.

4

AN UNCONDITIONAL SURRENDER

ACT I.

SCENE.—*The scene should represent windows, door, piazza, etc. A hotel front showing chairs scattered about. Door in centre of flat.* BELLE *seated in chair near entrance, reading a novel. A box of bon-bons on a chair beside her.*

BELLE. Ha! ha! ha! what perfect rubbish! (*she throws book down on chair by her*). (*Enter, as she does so,* DOLLY *and* MAY, *from centre door.*)

DOLLY. What's " perfect rubbish," dear?

BELLE. That! (*pointing scornfully to novel*).

MAY. (*seating herself on railing*) It must be delightful, I adore rubbish.

BELLE. This is worse than rubbish; it is libellous non-sense.

DOLLY. Upon whom? (*seating herself*).

BELLE. (*tragically*) Upon our sex!

MAY. (*eating a bon-bon*) Lovely! We deserve it all, dear.

BELLE. (*severely*) That from a woman! O May!

MAY. Why not? I'm sure I've been a positive source of unhappiness to at least a dozen people this day.

DOLLY. How?

MAY. (*reflectively*) Well, let me see. I asked pa this morning to bring me a diamond butterfly from Tiffany's for my *coiffure* for the ball at the West End next week.

DOLLY. That's *one !* (*holding up one finger as tally*).

MAY. And I ruined ma's lorgnette by sitting on it this noon.

DOLLY. (*holding two fingers*) That's two!

MAY. And I wrote an emphatic declination to Dickie Cruger's proposal of marriage received per the mail.

DOLLY. Beautiful! That's three. But tell us about Dickie.

BELLE. Yes, do!

MAY. Oh! dear me! There's nothing to tell. Dickie does it every once in a while. It's a weakness of his, poor boy! I know on positive evidence that he has offered his

5

heart to at least eight girls.   This is the fourth time he has honored me alone.

DOLLY.   Why don't somebody accept him and put him out of his misery?

MAY.   I'll write for him to come on.   Perhaps you will.

DOLLY.   Oh! dear no, sweet!   The season is too early yet.

BELLE.   But tell us more about Dickie.   Why does he propose so much?

MAY.   It's this way: His income is tied up by the will of his father, so that he can only draw so much every quarter. Well, every time the dear boy is flush he celebrates by proposing to one of " his girls," as he is pleased to call us.

DOLLY.   Sort of a mild dissipation.

BELLE.   It is really better than getting intoxicated.   He shows excellent taste.   But doesn't some girl accept him every now and then?

MAY.   Oh! yes; several have.

BELLE.   Several!   Why, he is a perfect Turk.

MAY.   You see, they didn't know Dickie.   He invariably breaks his engagements when his allowance runs low— which usually takes place about a month after he has drawn it.

DOLLY.   I wish he were here, after all.   I believe I would accept him under those circumstances.   Just think of the drives, bon-bons, and so on for the month!   Oh! it's just heavenly!

BELLE.   He must be utterly heartless, though.

MAY.   Not at all. He has *too* much heart to let love famish after a month of plenty.   He considerately gives some other man a chance.

BELLE.   Oh! I see.

DOLLY.   Well, dear, you have made three persons unhappy; who else?

MAY.   Tired of Dickie, already?   Well, let's see.   I told the bell boy he was as slow as treacle in the winter time when he went on an errand for me, and he actually looked hurt.

DOLLY.   That's four!

MAY.   And Mr. Van Artsdalen asked me to go out driving with him to-morrow and I declined, because I have been going too frequently with him of late.   He might be tempted to propose.

DOLLY.   The wretch!   He asked me to go driving, too: and I accepted.

MAY. When did he ask *you* ?

DOLLY. About eleven o'clock this morning.

MAY. Well, deary, you are playing second fiddle; he asked me at ten.

BELLE. Another one made unhappy!

DOLLY. Won't I make his life miserable for him on that drive. I think New York men are horribly deceitful!

MAY. (*with inflection*) Indeed!

DOLLY. He actually had the effrontery to intimate that he had been looking forward to driving with me for a week. The brute!

BELLE. I'm so glad you accepted his invitation, Doll. A second declination might have driven him to me, and *third* fiddle would have been simply unendurable. I should have been driven to melancholia.

DOLLY. I don't know but what I prefer that to being driven to Seabright with him. (*She bites a bon-bon savagely.*)

MAY. Why, dear, you are actually angry!

DOLLY. No; only mad!

BELLE. A distinction without a difference.

DOLLY. Pardon me; there is a difference.

MAY. What is it?

DOLLY. (*finishing the bon-bon with an emphatic craunch*) *I could bite him!!*

BELLE. Horrors! Will somebody please get a muzzle.

MAY. Oh! botheration! Let's drop the men and discuss something more profitable. You were speaking about that novel, Belle, when I interrupted you with my nonsense. What is it?

BELLE. Mr. Colfax's latest. Have you read it?

MAY. No. What is its title?

BELLE. *Miss Dawcett; A Modern Romance.*

DOLLY. Is it good?

BELLE. For nothing! Here's a sample (*picking up the book and reading in a melodramatic style*), "O Leon! my darling, you ask me if I am willing to give up all for love. You ask me *that!* When you know that if you should tell me to leap into the co-o-ld, dark sea I should do so, happy that I was dying at your behest. Leon, woman exists only for man. There is no value in living without some strong bosom on which to rest her timid, tender heart." Think of a man writing such truck as that and putting it into the mouth of the Nineteenth Century woman! Pah! It is sickening! (*She shuts the book, and tossing it down on the floor, puts her foot disdainfully on it.*)

MAY. I wonder where he gets his ideas of women from?

DOLLY. (*shyly*) Probably from New York, dear.   He lives there, doesn't he ?

MAY. Yes, my own ; but he was born in Philadelphia and spent his early life there.   His heroines are probably colored by his early impressions.

DOLLY.   Then his memory has been distorted by the years he has spent away from there.   The *mannishness* of the average New York maiden has probably driven him to the other extreme.

. MAY.   Dolly Mayfair, I consider that a libel upon the girls of my city.   I want you to remember that I am from New York.

DOLLY. (*pityingly*) Poor New York !

BELLE. (*holding up the bon-bon box*) There! There! You two are always fighting over your native cities.   It is really very bad form.   Sweeten up, dears, and confine your remarks to *Miss Dawcett* and its illustrious writer.   I think we girls owe it to our sex to enlighten him upon some things.

DOLLY.   What a delightful subject he will be for experimentation.   But you must count me out.   I'm afraid of him.

BELLE.   Afraid of *him ?*   Of a man !

DOLLY.   To be sure !   I'm not an Amazon.   He is so big and broad and distinguished that he quite overwhelms poor little me.

MAY.   Yes, but he has lovely eyes, and a perfect dream of a mustache ; and his voice—his voice—Oh ! it haunts me still !   (*Enter Mr. Colfax from door.*)

COLFAX. (*tossing the stump of a cigar onto the drive*) Whose voice has the honor of haunting Miss McCollum ?

MAY. (*sotto voce*) Mercy !   (*aloud*) Why—er—how you startled me !

COLFAX.   Awfully sorry.   Perhaps I had better go back and try it over again.   Maybe then I shall find out the name of the lucky individual whose voice haunts you.

DOLLY.   Ha! ha!   You are just as likely to find out if you stay.

BELLE.   Pray, how is it you have absented yourselves so long from the ladies since lunch ?

COLFAX.   A letter kept me, and, of course, the inevitable cigar, but the sound of your voices drew me even from that charmer.

BELLE. (*languidly*) That's rather lame, Mr. Colfax.   I notice your cigar—as usual—took precedence of the ladies. That is the way with you men.   And even now, I warrant, you only sacrificed the stump. A cigar has its limitations, like everything else.

COLFAX. (*smilingly stroking his mustache and lazily seating himself in a steamer chair*) Yes, Miss Walling; a cigar has its limitations. In that respect it is very much like woman.

BELLE. (*icily*) Ah! indeed! Pray tell us in what manner we women have the honor of resembling the weed.

COLFAX. Well, just as a cigar begins to grow really fascinating we men have to tear ourselves away from it or it singes our mustaches. You know, or, pardon me, you don't know, the sweetest part of a cigar to an old smoker is the stump. As with the cigar, so with woman. Just as one begins to enjoy the sweets of her society she grows dangerous by falling in love—and, presto! We men have to leave or suffer the consequences.

MAY. (*ingenuously*) Dear me! do women really fall in love nowadays? I thought all that nonsense was a thing of the past—or of novels (*demurely*).

COLFAX. Where do you get such ideas, my dear Miss McCollum? From the book that lies neglected at Miss Walling's feet? What is it? May I see?

BELLE. (*indifferently*) Really, what was I reading? Oh! yes, I remember! To be sure you may see it. (*She drags one slippered foot carelessly over it just as he stoops to pick it up.*)

COLFAX. How disdainfully you treat it. Who is the unfortunate author?—ah!—I see!

BELLE. (*maliciously*) Do you happen to know the book?

COLFAX. I think I have seen it somewhere. What do you think of it?

BELLE. (*critically*) It is printed on excellent paper.

COLFAX. Yes?

BELLE. And is well bound.

COLFAX. Again yes?

BELLE. And has some lovely illustrations.

COLFAX. The essentials having been so felicitously commented upon, what do you think of the unessential—the story?

BELLE. (*as if she had forgotten that part of the book*) Oh! the story! Well, it has a fair plot, is well punctuated and I haven't noticed any misspelled words, but—

COLFAX. Yes—" but "?

BELLE. But its heroine is an anachronism. There! As you've insisted on my judgment, you have it unglossed.

COLFAX. (*bowing*) And how, may I ask, is the heroine an anachronism?

BELLE. She is entirely too namby-pamby and wishy-washy for this age. The days of Fannie Burney's weeping Niobes have passed away forever. It is entirely out of date for your heroine to talk of dying for a man, or to declare that she exists only for his Royal Highness. If you will pardon a friend's frankness, Mr. Colfax, that is pure rubbishy sentimentalism.

COLFAX. (*arising with an extravagant gesture of mock despair*) I am crushed!—demolished!—flattened out into an unrecognizable novelist—and by a woman!—a frail, delicate woman! Ye gods! I am ruined! I shall never again dare to touch her. I shall have to write my next novel without a heroine—but—ha! (*tragi-comically*) has Miss Walling ever been in love?

BELLE. Mercy! I? In love? Dear me, never!

COLFAX. Then I really must decline to accept you as an authority on sentiment. If you have never been in love you are not a competent critic. How about that, Miss Mayfair? Am I not right?

DOLLY. (*humming*) "You are right, and Belle is right, and all is right as right can be."

MAY. (*biting another bon-bon*) By the way, Mr. Colfax, have you really ever been in love either?

BELLE. (*clapping her hands*) Bravo! May; bravo!

DOLLY. One good turn deserves another, Mr. Colfax. "The truth, the whole truth, and nothing but the truth!"

COLFAX. Frankly, ladies, no; never!

MAY. Then you—

DOLLY. Shouldn't write—

BELLE. About love!

COLFAX. (*addressing the heavens*) "Othello's occupation's gone!"

BELLE. I have a bright idea, Mr. Colfax.

COLFAX. Illumine me with it.

BELLE. If you really can't fall in love after a fair effort, get some one who has been through the mill to look after your heroines and their love affairs. In other words, a literary partner wouldn't be a bad idea for you.

MAY. A course in the School of Love, under Professor Cupid, would be the best, though.

COLFAX. *Mirabile dictu!* A Daniel come to judgment. Miss Walling, your suggestion does you credit. I will act upon it in my very next work. But I must away to my

desk. Fourteen letters to write and a story for *Harpers* before midnight. *Adios!*

BELLE. Adieu.

MAY. Must you go!

DOLLY. Farewell. (*Exit Mr. Colfax—door.*)

MAY. He's delicious!

DOLLY. He's sweet!

BELLE. Stuff! He's spoiled, and by women, too.

DOLLY. What a noble work it will be to unspoil him!

MAY. Glorious! but how?

BELLE. Take the conceit out of him! Cr—r—r—ush him!

MAY. The contract is yours, dear. Go in and win. (*Enter Mr. Pennington—right.*)

MR. PENN. (*excitedly*) Have any of you ladies seen Colfax?

BELLE. He has just gone to his rooms.

DOLLY Harry, what on earth's the matter with you? You look as if you had been in a fight.

MR. PENN. (*fiercely*) I have been insulted!

ALL. How? Why? By whom?

MR. PENN. (*shaking his fist at an imaginary enemy*) That scoundrel Van Artsdalen and I had some words about the speed of our horses, and he finally called me a—a liar!—me, a liar—think of it!

MAY. Well, what did you do then?

MR. PENN. (*wiping his face*) I called him another!

DOLLY. (*disappointedly*) Is that all? O Penny! the honor of Philadelphia is at stake.

MR. PENN. It is safe in my hands. It is pistols for two to-morrow morning at six!

BELLE. Mercy!

MAY. You're joking?

DOLLY. O Penn.! that's too much! Why don't you run your horses, or pitch pennies, or something.

MR. PENN. (*ferociously*) It is blood! b—l—o—o—d! Where's Colfax? He must be my second! (*Exit through door.*)

BELLE. Well, give me a man for foolishness!

DOLLY. It was contemptible, though, of Mr. Van Artsdalen to call Penn. a liar.

MAY. (*warmly*) I suppose he deserved it!

DOLLY. I don't believe he did. Penny's as truthful as the sunlight. Why, he's a Quaker!

MAY. And Ward's a New Yorker, I'd have you know.

DOLLY. Guilty on the first count!

MAY. Do you mean to insinuate, Miss Mayfair, that **a** New Yorker would tell an untruth?

DOLLY. (*stiffly*) I never insinuate.

MAY. (*hotly*) I beg your pardon, but you do!

DOLLY. (*hotly*) I beg *your* pardon, but I do *not!*

BELLE. Goodness, gracious! You girls are equal to two children. The next thing I'll have to second another duel. Peace! Peace! We must set our wits to work to keep these bloody-minded men from doing each other harm. (*Enter* MR. VAN ARTSDALEN—*left.*)

MR. VAN. (*excitedly*) Say, May, have you seen Colonel Lee about? I want him.

MAY. Not since lunch, Ward. What's the trouble?

MR. VAN. Why, that infernal ninny, Pennington, has called me a liar, and I am going to have his heart's blood!

BELLE. Oh! I wouldn't. It might kill him.

MR. VAN. (*fiercely*) The blood of the Van Artsdalens would turn to water in my veins if I did not wipe out this insult! I must find Lee. (*Exit door.*)

BELLE. (*in alarm*) It is getting serious. It would be dreadful if they should really come to blows.

MAY. Well, if the worst comes to the worst, I hope Ward won't get hurt.

DOLLY. And I hope Penn. wont get injured.

MAY. He deserves to be for being so ungentlemanly.

DOLLY. My compliments, and the same sentiments for Mr. Van Artsdalen!

BELLE. Dear me! What shall I do with such a lot of fire-eaters? I believe the whole world's gone wrong.

MAY. You haven't a particle of spunk.

DOLLY. You're neither flesh, fowl, nor good red herring!

BELLE. What have I done?

MAY. Why don't you sympathize with Ward? (*Walks away to right in a huff.*)

DOLLY. Why don't you sympathize with Penn.? (*Walks away to left in a huff.*)

BELLE. (*staring helplessly after each retreating form*) Well! well! What shall I do to restore peace? I must see Mr. Colfax, and at once. (*She starts to enter the door at the same moment that* MR. COLFAX *is coming out. Result, they run into each other.*)

BELLE. I beg your pardon! How you startled me!

COLFAX. Here's a pretty how d' ye do. These two silly chaps are bound to fight each other, and Penn. insists on my being his second! (*At the instant of this encounter,* MAY *at the right extreme and* DOLLY *at the left extreme of the piazza, walk into the arms of* MR. VAN. *and* MR. PENN. *respectively.*)

MAY. Mercy! how you frightened me!

MR. VAN. It is blood! But I can't find Lee anywhere.

MAY. I'll help you hunt for him. (*He and* MAY *go out— left.*)

DOLLY. (*at the other extreme*) Goodness! how you scared me.

MR. PENN. Ha! It is settled! To-morrow morning at six. Revolvers. Ten paces. (*Exeunt both—right.*)

(*N. B.—Action in all three collisions must be simultaneous ; dialogue consecutive.*)

COLFAX. (*remaining at the door with* BELLE) What is to be done if this frenzy keeps up ?

BELLE. If they insist on fighting, it must be with blank cartridges, of course.

COLFAX. That's the bother of the thing. Colonel Lee is an old war dog and he will probably insist that everything be done on the square. He'll be for tragedy, not comedy.

BELLE. Can't the police prevent it ?

COLFAX. Yes, if the worst comes to the worst. But think of the publicity. We should all figure in to-morrow's papers in a most ridiculous light.

BELLE. Horrors! but can't we get rid of the Colonel in some way ?

COLFAX. Ha! ha! we might kidnap him to-night.

BELLE. Why not send him a bogus telegram, summoning him home to New York before the duel comes off?

COLFAX. Beautiful! We'll do it! I know the name of his partner, and I'll sign his name to a dispatch that shall read thus: "The store is in flames. Come home at once."

BELLE. That will work, I am sure.

COLFAX. But what on earth will we do for a second for Van? He'll distrust me, because I am Penn.'s aid, and might insist on examining the weapons too closely if I attempted to act for both.

BELLE. Why, can't I take the Colonel's place ?

COLFAX. (*amused*) You?

BELLE. Yes ; why not? We'll bribe Eddie to deliver the dispatch in time to get the Colonel off on the 5.15 train in the morning, and I shall appear on the scene opportunely and offer my services—reluctantly, of course—at your suggestion.

COLFAX. Have you the nerve to carry it out ?

BELLE. Try me. Why I am positively not even afraid of a mouse.

COLFAX. Ha! ha! That is sufficient proof.

BELLE. Those belligerent fellows must be kept apart this evening. In their present state they are likely to disgrace us at any moment.

COLFAX. Can't Miss Mayfair and Miss McCollum be trusted to look after them?

BELLE. Oh! dear no! They are as eager for war as the men. It's New York *versus* Philadelphia, and you know what that means. Why, they are even down on poor me because I don't sympathize with their different opinions.

COLFAX. Well, I'll go and attend to the bogus dispatch and the bell boy, and leave you to look after the warring factions.

BELLE. Mercy! The responsibility overwhelms me! But I'll do my best. Good-bye!

COLFAX. Farewell! (*Exit door.*) (*Loud conversation is heard to right.*)

BELLE. I wonder who is coming? Such a chatter of tongues! (*Enter* MAY *and* MR. VAN ARTSDALEN, *both talking excitedly.*)

BELLE. (*with gesture of despair*) The engagement has begun!

MAY. (*to* WARD) Ward Van Artsdalen, the honor of New York rests upon you to-morrow. You must be worthy of your ancient name, and conquer the ignoble Quaker!

MR. VAN. (*raising his hand aloft*) I will! I will! By George, May, I shall punch his nose if I meet him. To-morrow is too far away.

MAY. (*rapturously*) Oh! aren't you lovely? I'm so sorry I declined going driving with you to-morrow; and to think you asked that deceitful little minx, Dolly Mayfair!

MR. VAN. 'Twas Hobson's choice—you wouldn't and she would. But I suppose the drive's off now.

MAY. Why?

MR. VAN. (*tragically*) I may be cold in death!

MAY (*bursting into tears*) Don't, Ward! You can't mean it!

MR. VAN. You don't suppose we are doing this thing for fun, do you?

MAY. (*sobbing*) Oh! I didn't really think you would shoot each other with real bullets.

MR. VAN. (*with sarcasm*) What did you expect us to use? Pea-shooters?

MAY. (*convulsively*) No—o—o! but you could shoot up in the air, like they do in the plays. It would be so noble and magnanimous!

MR. VAN. Fiddlesticks! Magnanimous with that fellow! He don't know the meaning of the word. No, May; either he or I must redden the sands of the shore with our blood.

MAY. (*catching sight of* BELLE *at the entrance*) O Belle! what shall we do? Ward and Mr. Pennington are in dead earnest. It's dreadful! I don't want anybody killed!

BELLE. Mr. Van Artsdalen do be forgiving!

MAY. Yes, do!

MR. VAN. Neve–r–r–r!

BELLE. (*sotto voce*) Suppose they meet in this frame of mind! There will be bloodshed sure. I must get him away. I wonder if he can be intimidated? (*Aloud*) Mr. Van Artsdalen, I wouldn't advise you to spend much time around here just now.

MR. VAN. Why not, pray? (*boldly.*)

BELLE. Mr. Pennington is looking for you with a six-shooter. He declares he won't wait till to-morrow. And I know from positive evidence he's a dead shot.

MAY. (*nervously*) O Ward! Ward! He may be aiming at you now from somewhere!

MR. VAN. (*dodging*) He wouldn't murder me, would he?

BELLE. He's a dangerous man when he is aroused.

MAY. Ward, go to your room, do! There's a dear good fellow. Mercy! What is that? I hear *his* voice! Go!

BELLE. (*pushing him*) Yes; go! Quick!! (MR. VAN. *rushes through door.*) (*Enter, left,* DOLLY *and* MR. PENNINGTON.)

DOLLY. (*to* PENN.) You musn't show the white feather, or all Philadelphia shall know your shame.

MR. PENN. (*boldly*) You know me well enough for that, Dolly.

DOLLY. To think of calling you a liar!

MR. PENN. (*with rising wrath*) Only to think! By Gad! I could wring his neck, the villain!

DOLLY. I shall be on hand to witness the encounter.

MR. PENN. 'Twill be no place for women.

DOLLY. Why not?

MR. PENN. (*gloomily*) Suppose I am killed!

DOLLY. Ugh! Don't! I hadn't thought of that.

MR. PENN. Well, I had. You don't imagine we are jesting, do you?

DOLLY. Jesting? No; but I didn't think you would try to kill each other.

MR. PENN. (*sardonically*) Ha! ha! ha! What'd you expect us to do? Throw sand in each other's eyes and then cry "Quits"?

DOLLY. (*in tears*) Oh! If you are really serious, I don't think I want you to fight!

MR. PENN. (*to the heavens*) Give me a woman for consistency! Here you've been egging me on, Dolly Mayfair, and now you want me to back down!

DOLLY. (*sobbing*) Well, you both might be killed—and that would be dreadful!

MR. PENN. (*gloomily*) If I fall, Dolly, will you write to my parents that I died for the honor of my city?

DOLLY. (*with fresh sobs*) Yes—y-e—s—Penny. I w-i—ll; but cu—cu—couldn't you sa-sa—save—the city's ho—ho—honor in some o-o—other way!

MR. PENN. (*tragically*) No! By heavens, it is blood and blood alone will wipe the stain away!

DOLLY. (*spying* MAY *and* BELLE *in entrance*) O girls! it is horrible! They're going to kill each other! Can't we prevent it in some way?

MAY. (*sobbing afresh*) Oh! Mr.—Mr.—Pen—Pen—Pennington, do be merciful.

BELLE. Yes, do, and we girls will adore you.

DOLLY. Yes—yes—please do, Penny,—tha—tha—that's a de—de—dear, good fellow!

MR. PENN. (*grandly*) The tears of women are of no avail where honor is at stake!

BELLE. (*sotto voce*) I must take the wind out of his sail, too. (*Aloud*) Mr. Pennington, with the permission of the ladies, I would like a word with you in private.

MR. PENN. A dozen, if you like. (*They step a few paces away.*)

BELLE. As a friend, I would advise you not to show yourself much around here before the duel.

MR. PENN. I should like to know why. Do you imagine I fear my antagonist? That! for him! (*Snapping his fingers.*)

BELL. He is armed with a six-shooter, and he was here just a moment ago vowing vengeance on you. He will shoot you on sight if he gets the chance. I *really* don't feel safe standing by your side. He is a dead shot, too. You had better get to your room and not appear till time for the duel.

MR. PENN. (*nervously looking over his shoulder*) I—I didn't think he was such a fiend!

BELLE. Oh! he's a perfect fire-eater. Be wise while it is yet time. Hark! I hear a step! Go!—for your life! (MR. PENN. *darts to left and disappears.*) (*Enter, door,* MR. COLFAX.)

COLFAX. Everything is arranged.

BELLE. I am so glad you have returned! I have had my hands full keeping those mad men apart.

MAY. It is horrible!

DOLLY. It is dreadful!

BELLE. Dears, you had both better go to your rooms. It must not appear that we have had anything to do with the wretched affair. Just suppose it should get into the papers!

MAY. Horrors!

BELLE. And your eyes are all red with weeping; you will attract attention. Do be sensible, both of you, and go!

DOLLY. My head is bursting; I guess I will take your advice.

MAY. And I, too. (*Exeunt both, centre.*)

BELLE. (*fetching a long breath*) There! They're all gone. Oh! what a strain my poor nerves have been on! And I have told some dreadful fibs!

COLFAX. (*smiling*) They were for a good cause, no doubt. How did you manage the men?

BELLE. Told each one that the other was hunting for him with a six-shooter. The way they sought cover was killing; I could have roared only for the woebegone faces of Dolly and May. The fight is all out of the quartette. The duel will be a perfect farce. Ha! ha! ha!

COLFAX. Unless Colonel Lee's telegram fails to do its work.

BELLE. That would be awful! It mustn't! I shall get up at four o'clock to-morrow morning and see that Eddie does his duty.

COLFAX. You are an admirable woman. I forgive you for handling my book without gloves.

BELLE. Has a word to the wise been sufficient?

COLFAX. It has. After the duel—ha! ha! ha!—I want to speak with you further in reference to that partnership which you were brilliant enough to suggest. But the duel is paramount now. Remember, to-morrow morning at six, on the mile beach. Till then, adieu! (*Exit MR. C.—right.*)

BELLE. (*looking after him*) He's not such a bad fellow, after all. His one fault is that he doesn't understand women (*striking a serio-comic attitude*), and mine shall be the duty to enlighten him! (*A bell rings loudly.*) Mercy! the dinner bell! and I'm not dressed. I must fly!! (*Exit—left.*)

(*Curtain.*)

2

ACT II.

SCENE.—*Should represent a strip of sandy beach with the ocean stretching away in the background. The ribs of an old wreck project above the sand to right and a sand-dune with patches of coarse grass and bay plants growing on it, to left.*

(*Enter, left,* BELLE *and* MR. COLFAX, MR. C. *carrying a hand-bag.*)

COLFAX. Thank heavens! the Colonel is off to New York. I followed him to the depot to make sure that he took the train.

BELLE. Glorious! Have you attended to the loading of the revolvers with blanks?

COLFAX. Ha! ha! ha! Yes; the deadly missiles are in place.

BELLE. I wonder if the duelists will really appear?

COLFAX. I think so, but I imagine they are both heartily sick of the whole business. They haven't showed their faces since yesterday afternoon.

BELLE. Ha! ha! each one regards the other as an assassin, thanks to my fibs.

COLFAX. Ah! there comes Harry Pennington, and yes—by George! Dolly Mayfair with him. (*Enter, left,* MR. PENN. *and* DOLLY.)

COLFAX. Well, my boy, you're on time, I see. Nerves all right?

PENNINGTON. Er—er—where's my adversary?

COLFAX. He hasn't honored us with his presence yet.

PENN. (*brightening*) Do you think he will show the white feather?

COLFAX. (*cheerfully*) No, he'll be here, I'm sure.

BELLE. Yes, there he comes with May.

DOLLY. O Harry!

PENN. (*gloomily*) 'Twill soon be over! (*Enter right,* MR. VAN ARTSDALEN *with* MAY.)

COLFAX. (*cheerfully*) Well, here we all are!

PENN. (*sardonically*) Colfax is as cool as if it were a song and dance show instead of a duel. It's none of his funeral, that's the reason.

DOLLY. I think he is detestable, and there is Belle Wall-

18

ing actually smiling at some remark of his! She is utterly
heartless!

VAN A. (*stopping near the wreck*) Er—er—where is the
Colonel?

COLFAX. He received a dispatch before five this morning that his store in New York was in flames and he just
had time to make the train. He sent his regrets and wished
you the best kind of luck.

PENN. (*aside to* DOLLY) The Colonel's excessively
kind!

VAN. A. But who is to be my second?

MAY. You mustn't think of fighting without one!

DOLLY. (*eagerly*) No, indeed!

COLFAX. How would Miss Walling do in the emergency?

VAN A. Miss Walling! She is only a woman!

BELLE. Any port in a storm. Mr. Van Artsdalen, you
surely won't disappoint Mr. Pennington by refusing to fight,
for such a trifle as the absence of your expected second?

MAY. (*sotto voce*) The shameless thing!

VAN A. (*desperately*) All right! anything to end the sus-
pense.

COLFAX. Very well! To your positions, gentlemen.
The sun is on your side so there is no choice. (MR. VAN A.
and MR. PENN. *take their places, the one by the wreck the other
by the dune.*) Gentlemen, this is to be a duel at ten paces,
if I remember rightly, not a thousand yards, more or less.
Let me step it off. (*He does so.*) There! Mr. Van Artsdalen,
you will stand at this line, and Mr. Pennington at this.

PENN. Er—it seems to me that is pretty close.

COLFAX. (*sternly*) You are going to fight with revolvers,
not long range cannon, aren't you?

PENN. (*weakly*) Ye-es.

COLFAX. Well, let us have no further parleying, but get
down to business. Miss Walling, the weapons, please!
(BELLE *opens the bag and takes out the revolvers.*)

MAY. · Ugh!

DOLLY. Ugh! (*They retreat together to front of dune.*)

COLFAX. That's right, ladies. Get well out of range, the
bullets might miss their mark and hit one of you.

MAY. Mercy!

DOLLY. Oh! Oh! (BELLE *hands one revolver to* MR.
COLFAX *and retains the other.*)

COLFAX. Gentlemen, your weapons are ready. (*He and*
BELLE *advance to their respective principals and offer the revolvers.*) ·

PENN. (*weakly*) Thanks!

VAN. (*weakly*) Thanks! (*The seconds take positions toward sea on the far side of the duelists.*) (MAY *and* DOLLY *are sobbing convulsively and are looking through their fingers at the preparations being made for the bloody work.*)

DOLLY. Oh! They—they—are re—re—ready to shoot!

MAY. I won—wo—wonder which one will be ki—ki—killed?

DOLLY. Bo—bo—bo—both of them ma—ma—may be!

MAY. And that ter—ter—terrible author is—is—smiling as if—he—were go—go—going to be married! ·

DOLLY. And Be—Be—Belle is lo—lo—looking as pleased as—if—she—were—the—the bride!

MAY. Mercy! they're aiming! (*She and* DOLLY *bury their faces on each other's shoulders and put their fingers in their ears.*)

COLFAX. I will count ten and as I pronounce the last number you will both fire. Are you ready? One! two! three!

PENN. Stop a moment! Suppose neither bullet hits the er—er—mark; what will we do?

COLFAX. (*inflexibly*) Go right on shooting till one or the other of you falls. Four! Five! Six—

VAN. Stop! Suppose we are both er—er—killed at the first fire; what then?

COLFAX. (*sternly*) Then you will both cease firing. Seven! Eight! Nine!—

PENN. (*in great agitation*) Hold up! I forgot to leave any last words for my poor dear mother (*choking*).

COLFAX. It isn't customary to stop the proceedings at this stage, but we'll make an exception this time. Go ahead!

PENN. Tell her I—I—died with my face to the foe—and that my last thoughts were of her—and tell my sister—my poor, dear sister—who won't have any brother when I am gone—

MAY and DOLLY. (*by the dune*) Boo hoo—hoo—hoo!

PENN. That I died with my heart full of love for her—and tell my father, my dear old father who will miss me so much—that I fell with the fame of the Pennington's unsullied—and tell my blessed grandmother that I little thought that when I said "good-bye" to her I should never—see her again—

DOLLY and MAY. Boo hoo—hoo—hoo!

PENN. And tell my Grandfather Biddle that I have always loved and venerated him more than any other grandfather I have ever had, and tell my Aunt Serena that—

COLFAX. See here, Pennington, if you are going through the whole family tree, I had better send for a stenographer!

PENN. (*eagerly*) Yes, do! I'm not near through yet.

COLFAX. Can't wait any longer, old boy. It's getting near breakfast time, and I'm famishing.

DOLLY. The brute!

COLFAX. Now, look out, Te—!

VAN. (*excitedly*) Hold on just a moment longer! I want to express a wish as to what shall be done with a few of my valuables if you will kindly remember them.

COLFAX. (*resignedly*) Certainly, old fellow, anything to oblige. But make it short. I smell liver and onions from somewhere.

MAY. The wretch. (BELLE *with great difficulty is restraining her laughter.*)

VAN. Well, to my mother I leave my shares of Reading and my Government four per cents., and the Chemical Bank stock. To my Brother Frank I give and bequeath my stable of thoroughbreds—my cart and my brougham—and my dogs. To my elder sister Kate my shares of Manhattan " L " stock and my diamond scarf-pins. To my younger sister, Nell, I bequeath my money on deposit in the Chemical and my pet owl, Dodo—

MAY and DOLLY (*afresh*). Boo—hoo—hoo—hoo—

VAN. To my Uncle George I give my cabinet of rare coins and my pipes. To his wife, my Aunt Eleanor—my old china. To my—

COLFAX. See here, gentlemen, I really can't wait any longer. I shall simply die of starvation. Come, now! get ready! quick! (*Both duelists groan, raise the revolvers and shut their eyes.* DOLLY *and* MAY *drop to the ground and huddle into each other's arms.*) Now, ten! (*Both fire.* BANG! BANG!) (*Both fall to the ground and continue firing wildly straight up in the air until all the chambers are exhausted.*)

DOLLY. O—o—o—h!!

MAY. O—o—o—o—h!!

COLFAX. (*shouting*) Come, come, come! You'll rouse all New Jersey. You've done all the harm you can, now stop!

MR. VAN. I die! I die!

MR. PENN. I perish! I perish! Farewell, my poor old mother!

COLFAX. (*running to* PENN. *and shaking him, while* VAN. *continues to groan,* DOLLY *and* MAY *to weep, and* BELLE *to stuff the handkerchief in her mouth*) Stuff and nonsense, Harry! you're all right! Get up and be a man, or I'll have to punch your head.

MR. PENN. Eh? eh? What! Aint I killed?

COLFAX. Killed, fiddlesticks! you're worth a carload of dead men yet. Why you are not even wounded. Up you go! (*giving him a lift to a sitting posture.*)

BELLE. (*running to* MR. VAN. *and shaking him also*) Mr. Van Artsdalen, do for mercy's sake stop that dreadful noise, and get up! You're not hurt.

MR. VAN. (*opening his eyes*) I'm dead!

BELLE. So am I—about as much! Come! Stir yourself, or I shall cease to respect you.

MR. VAN. Aint I hit somewhere?

BELLE. No! No! Not a scratch, not a hair on your mustache turned even. Sit up! (*He does so.*)

MR. VAN. (*staring at his opponent*) Is he hurt?

BELLE. Not a bit.

MR. VAN. (*drawing a long breath*) By George, I'm glad! Helloa, Penny!

MR. PENN. Helloa, Van!

COLFAX. Get up and shake hands like good fellows. You fought well—now make up nobly!

MR. PENN. Van!

MR. VAN. Penny! (*They fall upon each other's necks and embrace fervently.*)

DOLLY. (*peeping over* MAY's *shoulder*) Oh! mercy! they're not dead after all! They're—they're—why they're actually embracing each other!

MAY. (*staring*) Well, I never did!

DOLLY. Neither did I! (*They arise and timidly approach the duelists and seconds.*)

BELLE. (*laughing*) Isn't it glorious, girls? The honor of New York and of Philadelphia is saved and not a drop of blood spilled!

MAY. Lovely!

DOLLY. Perfect! (MAY *and* DOLLY *also embrace rapturously.*)

COLFAX. (*laughing*) We're not in fashion, Miss Walling. We shall at least have to shake hands.

BELLE. (*laughing*) "Everybody is happy and the goose hangs high." (*They shake hands.*)

COLFAX. I'll wager they're cured of dueling.

BELLE. To their dying day!

MR. PENN. (*emerging smiling from the arms of* MR. VAN. *and looking at the sky*) Ah! Isn't it a lovely day? I didn't appreciate it before.

MR. VAN. (*taking a long breath*) I thought my lungs had lost their job. Ah! that sea breeze is glorious!

MAY. (*approaching*) Van, you did nobly!

DOLLY. (*approaching*) Penny, you're a hero!

MR. PENN. (*modestly*) I don't feel like one.

MR. VAN. What asses we were!

MR. PENN. Amen!

BELLE. "Let the dead past bury its dead." We've an hour before breakfast. Let's sit here and enjoy this lovely air, while we are regaining our composure.

MAY. My complexion will be ruined in this sun.

DOLLY. I'll look like a speckled egg if I stay here another half hour.

BELLE. I ordered Eddie to bring our parasols and some sandwiches at seven. He ought to be here pretty soon.

MR. PENN. (*with dignity*) Miss Walling, you seem to have regarded this affair as a picnic!

BELLE. (*roguishly*) Oh! I knew neither one of you could hit a barn.

MR. VAN. Why, you told me yesterday Penn was a dead shot!

MR. PENN. And you told me that Van. was, too.

COLFAX. (*laughing*) "Be sure your sin will find you out," Miss Walling!

BELLE. (*desperately*) I told those fibs to keep you men from disgracing yourselves publicly.

MR. PENN. By George! We did make fools of ourselves, Van., didn't we?

MR. VAN. (*sadly*) I'm afraid we did, Penny.

BELLE. But really I knew you couldn't hit anything. I saw you both practicing at different times in the shooting gallery, and you could neither one of you come within a yard of the target.

MR. VAN. I guess you're about right. That's the reason I thought I was good for a funeral when I heard that Penn. was a dead shot.

MR. PENN. Same way here, old man.

BELLE. (*aside to* MR. COLFAX) Shall we tell them the jo on them about the blank cartridges?

COLFAX. (*aside*) Not for worlds! Let that be a secret between us forever.

DOLLY. Stop your whispering, you two there! Here comes that dear Eddie! (*Enter* EDDIE, *right, with basket and parasols.*)

MAY. (*to* EDDIE) You jewel you! I'm starving!

EDDIE. (*showing his teeth*) Yeth'm! Hyars somefin' sabe yo' life, den, sho'. Yah! yah! yah! (*Exit.*)

COLFAX. Ha! ha! ha! He's a comical genius. (*Opening the basket.*)

BELLE. That laugh of his is a sure cure for the blues. (*Passing the parasols.*)

MR. PENN. (*contentedly*) What a glorious thing it is to be alive! (*Taking a sandwich.*)

MR. VAN. I never appreciated living before. (*Doing the same.*)

COLFAX. This is high living. (*Biting a sandwich.*) (*The group sits on sand sideways to the audience in sprawling seashore fashion. The sun is supposed to be oceanward, hence the parasols will slant that way and every action can be seen by audience.*)

COLFAX. (*digging in sand*) Miss Walling, I feel like a boy to-day! Shall I make you a back rest? (*Piling up the sand behind her.*)

BELLE. You lovely man!

MR. PENN. Singular thing, but I feel uncommonly gay. One would suppose I should feel dreadfully sober after the "late unpleasantness," but I don't.

COLFAX. Reaction, my boy!

DOLLY. The same principle, I suppose, that makes me want to giggle and laugh and cut up outrageously the very moment a funeral is over.

MR. VAN. Please don't mention funerals. I don't want even to read the obituaries in the papers for the next ten years.

DOLLY. Oh! do let me have our dear old *Public Ledger* sent you from Philadelphia. It's like going through a cemetery to read its obituary page—epitaphs and all are there.

MR. PENN. (*reciting*) " We had a little Willie once,
     He was our joy and pride,
     But ah! he was too frail for earth,
     For soon he slept and died."

DOLLY. " Gone to meet his step-mother."

MR. VAN. Stop! stop! I'm in a cold perspiration already.

MR. PENN. Well, to change the subject, I've noticed a singular thing about my hair.

COLFAX. That you haven't much?

MR. VAN. That it isn't your own?

MR. PENN. No! but every time I come to the seashore, instead of having beautiful brown locks I have sandy hair inside of twelve hours. (*The whole party collapses with melancholy groans.*)

MR. VAN. (*faintly*) Penny!

MR. PENN. (*proudly*) Anything I can do for you, my boy?

MR. VAN. (*still more faintly*) Water!

MR. PENN. (*tragically*) Ha! what my bullets failed to do my pun has accomplished. 'Tis well!

COLFAX. (*sitting up and breathing hard*) Don't! old man, don't! or, like Sampson, you will slay your thousands.

MR. VAN. And with one of Sampson's weapons, too.

MAY. What's that?

MR. VAN. (*preparing to flee*) The jaw-bone of an—

MR. PENN. Villain! (*He grapples* MR. VAN., *and they tussle until they both fall exhausted at the feet of the ladies.*)

BELLE. Please, do stop. It makes me warm to look at you.

MAY. (*sternly*) Ward Van Artsdalen, there is no one to hold my parasol!

MR. VAN. (*throwing himself beside her, meekly*) Thy slave is here.

MR. PENN. Your fate warns me in time. (*He reclines beside* DOLLY.)

COLFAX. Miss Walling, let's look for shells.

BELLE. Very well. (*The two get up and exit right, leaving the two couples under the parasols. Some very effective by-play now begins.* DOLLY *and* MR. PENN. *are seated toward the dune,* MAY *and* MR. VAN. *toward the wreck. Gradually the two men shift the parasols so that they are partially shut off from each other's view. Before things culminate, an alternating dialogue takes place as follows :*)

MR. PENN. Dolly, don't you think that parasol had better be moved a little? The sun seems to be inquisitive.

DOLLY. You are holding the handle, Penny. Upon you rests the responsibility of keeping me in the shade.

MR. PENN. (*shifting it well around so as to shut out* MR. VAN. *and* MAY) I accept the responsibility manfully. (*He settles down cozily beside her in such a way that she is nearest the audience, and owing to the position of the parasol, facing toward the dune. There is a brief silence in which some little pantomime may be enacted of a tentatively lover-like nature, while* MR. VAN. *is going through a similar manœuvre with the parasol and his companion.*)

MR. VAN. May, have you noticed how the sunshine falls on that distant steeple? (*pointing to right at an object supposedly in their line of vision*).

MAY. (*shifting her position so as to see what he is pointing to*) Isn't it lovely! Why, what a beautiful perspective there is from this point of view.

MR. VAN. (*bringing the parasol around so as to screen himself and* MAY *from the view of the others*) By George,

May, I feel perfectly happy, somehow or other. (*He nestles down by her further side, and there is silence and pantomime.*)

MR. PENN. (*resuming*) Dolly, are you glad that I was un-injured in the—er—duel?

DOLLY. What a foolish question to ask me, Penny! You know that I am.

MR. PENN. Suppose I had died, would you have missed me?

DOLLY. O Penny! (*Eloquent silence and more pantomime.*)

MR. VAN. (*resuming*) May, why did you decline my invitation to drive yesterday. Have you grown tired of my attentions?

MAY. O Ward! I was just a little out of sorts yesterday. To be sure I haven't grown tired of you! You must surely know me better than that.

MR. VAN. If I had been killed would you have felt sorry?

MAY. Ward, don't even speak of it! (*Silence and pantomime.*)

MR. PENN. Dolly, what a beautiful hand you have. (*He takes it; she attempts to draw it away, but he holds fast.*)

DOLLY. You are holding what doesn't belong to you!

MR. PENN. (*innocently*) Why, you asked me to hold your parasol for you.

DOLLY. I refer to my hand. (*She again attempts to withdraw it.*)

MR. PENN. 'Tis such a little thing. I wish it were mine! (*Silence again and pantomime.*)

MR. VAN. May, I want to thank you for the noble way you stood by me through the late trouble.

MAY. And I want to congratulate you that you came through it all so grandly.

MR. VAN. I do not regret the duel at all.

MAY. Why, Ward!

MR. VAN. It has made me realize more fully how sweet and lovely you are.

MAY. Oh! (*Silence, etc., etc.*)

MR. PENN. Dolly, your sweet sympathy and encouragement have been more fatal to me than Van.'s bullets.

DOLLY. (*softly*) Have they?

MR. PENN. (*kissing her hand*) Dear, will you give me this little hand forever?

DOLLY. What would I do without it?

MR. PENN. O darling! you must go with the hand. (*Desperately*) Dolly, I love you!

DOLLY. This is so sudden!

MR. PENN. But none the less sweet, is it, dear?

DOLLY. No-o—o. (*Silence and eloquent pantomime.*)

MR. VAN. Darling! I–I—

MAY. Ward, you forget yourself!

MR. VAN. (*desperately*) I forget words! May, I—, will you be mine? (*Taking her hand.*)

MAY. Your duel has driven you crazy! (*Attempting to withdraw her hand.*)

MR. VAN. Dear, I love you! There! May I hope even a little bit?

MAY. (*drooping her head*) Ye–es, dear! (*Eloquent silence and pantomime. The silence under the parasols becomes complete: all the pantomime action that the nature of the situations suggest is in order. Enter BELLE and MR. COLFAX, right background, talking.*)

COLFAX. Miss Walling, I am going to ask an extraordinary thing of you.

BELLE. You alarm me.

COLFAX. You are to blame. You suggested a literary partner to help me in my next novel. Will you be that partner?

BELLE. I? You are jesting!

COLFAX. I was never more serious. Please say yes.

BELLE. Ha! ha! ha! That is the most ridiculous proposition to which I have ever listened. I can't write at all!

COLFAX. You needn't write much. You can criticise and suggest, and look after the love-making in the story.

BELLE. Charming plan! But I am not an authority in love, as you remarked yesterday.

COLFAX. You are a woman and a woman may learn intuitively what a man could never acquire except by actual experience. I have set my heart on your consenting to my plan. Do not disappoint me.

BELLE. Very well, I agree; you must be responsible for all the consequences of your foolhardy proposition.

COLFAX. I accept them all. Then that is settled. We will begin this very afternoon.

BELLE. Very well. But isn't it nearly breakfast time?

COLFAX. (*taking out his watch*) Five minutes of eight.

BELLE. (*turning and catching sight of the parasols*) That looks serious. They have shut us out in the cold.

COLFAX. The duel has brought things to a head, evidently. Oh! Cupid has strange ways.

BELLE. We must disturb those parasols if we want a hot breakfast!

COLFAX. (*throwing some sand against them*) Hey, Penny! Van! Ladies! Breakfast!

MR. VAN. (*in muffled tones*) Throw breakfast to the dogs!

MR. PENN. Bother breakfast!

BELLE. (*reciting*) "We can live without love; what is love but repining?
> But where is the man who can live without dining?"

Come, girls, I am approaching; I shall confiscate those sunshades. (MR. PENN. *and* MR. VAN. *hastily remove their arms from around the waists and their heads from the shoulders of their respective sweethearts.*)

BELLE. (*ruthlessly removing the protecting shade from each and shaking her finger at them*) You've been making love!

MAY. How do you know?

BELLE. Your hair is tumbling down.

DOLLY. (*springing up*) Don't mind her, May. Another case of sour grapes.

BELLE. (*throwing a handful of sand at* DOLLY) Wretch!

DOLLY. (*returning sand*) There!

COLFAX. (*sniffing the air*) I smell ham! I must away!

MR. PENN. So do I. (*Sotto voce to* DOLLY) I am starving, my own!

DOLLY. (*reproachfully*) How can you be if you really love me?

MR. PENN. Dear, I—(*he is interrupted by a handful of sand, thrown by* MR. VAN., *striking him in the back.*)

MR. PENN. (*wildly*) Who threw that? Show me the villain.

MR. VAN. I, sirrah, am he! What have you to say to it?

MR. PENN. Pistols and coffee for two. Prepare to die! (*He points his finger at* MR. VAN.)

MR. VAN. Beware, boaster! (*He points his finger at* MR. PENN.)

BELLE. Another duel!

COLFAX. Be quick! Fire!! (MR. PENN. *and* MR. VAN. *both say "bang!" "bang!" and fall stiffly back into the arms of their respective sweethearts.* BELLE *and* MR. COLFAX *take out handkerchiefs and pretend to weep.*)

(*Curtain falls on tableau.*)

ACT III.

SCENE I.—*Same as opening act.*

TIME.—*Three weeks later.*

(*Enter* MR. PENN.; *door.*)

MR. PENN. (*looking at diamond ring which he holds in his fingers and soliloquizing*) Well, my brief dream is ended! Three weeks of bliss—and now—despair! Yes, Dolly and I quarreled last night. Just a trifle started it, too—a simple remark of mine about May looking really beautiful in her new gown is to blame. What was there in that? Can't a man speak of another woman when he is engaged? By George! Love is a queer plant. It wants all the sunshine and the dew the heart can give, and will permit no single ray of friendship or admiration to fall on any other soil. Like Oliver Twist, Love sups and still cries "More!" I have put my heart in the Bank of Love, and the first quarrel has made a run upon it sufficient to bankrupt it. Confound it! I shall turn cynic and drink gall! I shall become a woman-hater and bury myself in a hermitage! Love is a melodrama and the actors are cheats! Jealousy is the villain—the first quarrel the prompter—and hate rings down the curtain on the last act. Bah! I'm done with it forever!
(*Enter* MR. VAN ARTSDALEN, *door.*)

MR. VAN. (*tragically*) Penn, I am going to kill myself!

MR. PENN. (*putting the ring hastily in his pocket*) What's up?

MR. VAN. All's up! May has thrown me over. The game's ended and I've lost.

MR. PENN. (*sympathetically*) You don't say so! Why, old fellow, I'm in exactly the same boat. Dolly and I have separated forever.

MR. VAN. (*tragically*) They have trifled with us both! Let them beware!

MR. PENN. (*gloomily*) What's to be done?

MR. VAN. (*desperately*) I shall shoot myself in her presence and expire at her feet!

MR. PENN. Nonsense! I wouldn't give her that satisfaction.

MR. VAN. Satisfaction?

29

MR. PENN. Exactly. Shoot yourself for a woman, and she'll shed a tear, say "Poor fool! He loved me well." and forget you for the next suitor. Pshaw! We have been idiots! Let us be wise and abjure women forever!

MR. VAN. (*sadly*) I thought in May I had met my affinity.

MR. PENN. And I was sure Dolly was mine, but it seems that we were both mistaken.

MR. VAN. I suppose they are laughing at the two of us.

MR. PENN. Ha! I have an idea!

MR. VAN. What is it?

MR. PENN. I shall make desperate love to your late *fiancée* and you shall make love to mine.

MR. VAN. That's brilliant tomfoolery! What would be gained?

MR. PENN. Well, in the first place our ex-loves wouldn't have the satisfaction of seeing us mope. And in the second place, when a woman sees that a man can get along perfectly well without her, she begins to want him again.

MR. VAN. Where have you gotten your extraordinary insight into the female heart?

MR. PENN. Ha! ha! From long and careful study of the subject *au naturel*.

MR. VAN. There is wisdom in your observations. On second thought I agree. When shall we begin our campaign?

MR. PENN. At once.

MR. VAN. At once! How?

MR. PENN. We will each write a note asking the maiden of our choice to meet us, say at the rustic seat on the ocean lawn. Make the time of our appointments about half an hour apart, or long enough for me to stroll up the beach with May and give you a free field with Dolly; then you will start up the beach, too, and I will be coming back with May by that time. We will meet unconcernedly, make some flippant remarks, and pass on. 'Twill be beautiful! What disdain the maidens will cast upon each other and upon us! Come to my den and we will concoct the notes.

MR. VAN. Glorious! I can see it all. But, I say, old fellow, you will have to write both billets. I have a deucedly sore hand.

MR. PENN. All right. I've never had occasion to write a line to either of the girls before. My presence here continually has rendered love letters unnecessary.

MR. VAN. Same here. But come! Time is flying. They will be down soon for the afternoon. Penny, you are a Machiavelli. (*Exeunt both, door. Enter* BELLE, *from right.*)

BELLE. (*slowly walking with drooping head*) Why should love be an entering wedge for misery? Here are Dolly and May unhappy and Mr. Pennington and Mr. Van Arts-dalen wretched over their broken engagements, and I—I—Oh! why is he so blind. We have been writing of love together, and he, who knows naught about it, has taught me to adore him, while I, who know now all love's meaning, can teach him less than nothing. (*Enter* MR. COLFAX, *door.*)

BELLE. (*sotto voce*) Ah! there he is, and I must cover my love with simple friendship's mask! Good afternoon, Mr. Colfax.

COLFAX. Miss Walling, I have been searching every-where for you.

BELLE. (*gayly*) That is delightful. You know we women like to be sought after.

COLFAX. A pleasant weakness, which we men are not unwilling to encourage. What I wanted to see you about is to tell you that, owing to a little business at the Branch, I shall be unable to attend to any writing until four o'clock. At that hour I shall be at liberty to put, with your assistance, the finishing touches to our joint effort. Will the time suit?

BELLE. Any hour suits me; and, besides, 'twill give me more time to perfect that love scene from my point of view.

COLFAX. By the way, the course of true love has shown its proverbial crookedness with our mutual friends. Penny and Van. are looking as woebegone as fishes out of water, and I haven't been able to catch a glimpse of the ladies since the "hop" last evening. Are they really out for good?

BELLE. I trust it is only a lovers' quarrel; I shall try to act as mediator, if I can.

COLFAX. I wish you success. They have made excel-lent subjects for me to study these past three weeks. I have made considerable progress in my knowledge of love, ha! ha! ha!

BELLE. I'm afraid your knowledge even now is only surface deep. It don't come from the right source. Love is born in the heart, not outside.

COLFAX. (*smiling*) Whence this increase of heart lore on my fair Athena's part?

BELLE. ·A woman has more of intuition than a man. Perhaps that accounts for my wisdom.

COLFAX. Whatever the source, I am sure my, or rather our book will reap the benefit of your learning in the soulful finale. Adios for the present. (*Exit, door.*)

BELLE. (*bitterly*) Blind and heartless both! He speaks of love as flippantly as if it were a mere incident of life instead of the keystone of existence. Oh! that I could teach him the truth! The tortures of Tantalus are summer pastimes compared with those a woman endures who loves, and dares not let it be known. (*She sighs and walks to the left of piazza, and disappears.*) (*Enter* EDDIE, *the bellboy, door, with two envelopes in his hand. He looks in every direction, then seats himself in chair by door.*)

EDDIE. (*solil.*) I don' know whar dose ladies is. Not in der rooms—not yere. Reckon I'll done hab to set yere and wait fo' 'em. Mus' be 'ticlar impo'tant, cos Mistah Van Ars'len an' Mistah Penn'gton, done gib me half a dollah apiece fo' deliberin' dese yere 'pistles safe 'n sound. Yah! yah! Dem fellahs hab got it bad! Jes' nothing but billin' and cooin' round yere for two or tree weeks. Ef I goes out on de piaze aft' dark to straighten de cheers, dehs Mistah Penn'gton and Miss Mayfair a yum-yummin in some co'ner, or if I looks into de parlah and tink it's empty dehs Mistah Van Ars'len and Miss 'Collum a chewin' tooty-frooty on de sofa. I 'clar' to goodness, it's nuff to make dis niggah sick. (*Looks at letters.*) Ki yi! Golly! deys done fo'got to seal dese yer 'pistles up. Dis chile's gwine to see how dat white trash make lub. (*Takes the note out of one envelope and reads slowly.*) "Deah fren'"—humph! dat's a drefful po' way to 'gin a letter to a sweetheart! When I writes to Chloe I sez "my own beautifullest lub" or suthin' like dat. Guess I'll hab to gib dem fellahs some pin'tahs on writin' lub letters. Le's see ef dehs any ting bettah dan de startin' out. (*reads*) "Dear fren', you will be 'sprised to get dis note from me." (*solil.*) 'sprised! yah! yah! I 'specs deys a passin' ob 'em all de time when dey aint a huggin' and kissin an' a makin' sheep's eyes at one anudder. (*reads*) "you'll be 'sprised to get dis note from me, but I wants to see yo' on berry 'ticlar business." (*solil.*) Yah! mo' squeezin', I spec! "'tic'lar business, and I asks yo', as a favor, to meet me at half-past tree o'clock at de rustic bench. Yours trooly, Ward Van Ars'len." (*Laying letter on his lap and staring at it.*) Well, dat's mos' s'prisin' lub letter eber I see! I don' see no lub in dat, no mo'n nothin' at all. I wondah ef dis udder 'pistle am a de-provement on dis yere truck? (*Takes out second letter and reads.*) "Deah fren'." (*solil.*) Well, dese yere white folks ain' got no sense o' lub writin's. I guess "deah fren'" mus' be fash'nable. Yah! yah! Well yere's de res'. (*reads*) "Yo'll be 'sprised to get dis note from me, but I wants to see yo' on berry 'tic'lar business, and I asks yo', as a favor, to meet me at tree o'clock at de rustic bench. Yours trooly, Harry Pennington." Well, did yo' ebber in all yo' bo'n days! Does I see double, or does dey buy dese yere lub letters by de gross ready made? I clar to gracious! deys done bofe write 'em de eyedentical same way, han'writin' an' all, 'ceptin' dehs a half hour's dif'fence in de time. Well, dat gets my pimpernickle! Dese yere white folks am too much for dis niggah. Lub letters! Yah! yah! yah! Oh! my golly, deh comes Miss Mayfair! 'Specs I get my neck bruck, ef I don' get dese yere in fo' she gets yere! Crickey me! which am which? Sho! niggah, don' be a fool! ob cos', Mistah Penn'gton's writin' to Miss Mayfair an' Mistah Van Ars'len am to Miss 'Collum. (*Putting the wrong letters in the envelopes.*) 'Specs I'd bettah paste 'em up, too. Might tink dis niggah been readin' 'em. Yah! yah! (*He hastily seals them up and puts them in his pocket.*) (*Enter, left piazza,* DOLLY.)

DOLLY. (*with downcast face, slowly strolling*) Ah, me! What a little thing can change one's whole life. Just a few words and Harry and I are out forever! The world is a blank to me. I don't care whether I live or die. (*Throws out her hands with a gesture of despair.*)

EDDIE. (*sotto voce*) Hi, golly! Guess dat gal ain' a feelin' well way she's a pawin' de air!

DOLLY. (*solil.*) But pshaw! There are as good fish in the sea as ever came out of it! He's quick tempered or he would never have gotten so angry over my playfully objecting to his praising May. Just as if I cared a cent how much he praised her! Humph! I'll show him I can be as independent as he can. What is it, Eddie?

EDDIE. (*approaching and holding out the note*) Yere's a lettah, Miss, from a gemmelman what was berry 'tic'lar dat I should deliber it to yo' in pusson.

DOLLY. (*taking it eagerly*) Thanks, Eddie!

EDDIE. Yo' welcome, ma'am. (*Retiring to his chair.*)

DOLLY. (*strolling back the way she came and hastily tearing the envelope*) I wonder who this can be from? Do you suppose *he* can have had the temerity to write to me after last night's bitter words? (*Reads*) "Dear friend," oh! how cold that sounds! "You will be surprised to get this note from me, but I want to see you on very particular business, and I ask you, as a favor, to meet me at the rustic

bench at three o'clock. Yours truly, Harry Pennington."
(*solil.*) Meet him! What for, I wonder? To listen to more
of his cruel speeches? I'll not go! No! I shall treat this
with silent contempt. Does he think he can treat me as he
did last night and then whistle me back like a dog? But,
maybe he is sorry. Maybe I did seem jealous to him.
Poor boy! I wonder if he is suffering? This is such a
humble note. I—I—believe—I will grant him this one
favor. Three o'clock! Why, 'tis nearly that now. I must
hasten. (*She hums a song, and comes back to centre.*)
Thank you, Eddie, very much! Here's a quarter for you.

EDDIE. (*grinning*) Tank'ee, Missy! (*Exit* DOLLY.)
Yah! yah! yah! she am as chipper as a June bug. Wisht
deh war' jes' a dozen o' dem lubbers roun' yere, 'spec's I
could retiah from business pretty soon, den. I wondah
whar dat Miss 'Collum am? Deh she comes, as sho's yo's
bo'n. (*Enter* MAY, *right, slowly.*)

MAY. (*bitterly*) What a fool a woman is! To give her
heart to any man, thinking that 'twill be safe in his keeping
forever. Bah! 'twould be safer with dogs. A remark of
mine about Mr. Colfax's genius has turned Ward's love to
ice and mine to gall. Oh! I am miserable! (*She throws
out her arms as if in agony.*)

EDDIE. (*sotto voce*) I 'clar to gracious, Miss 'Collum am a
feelin' bad, too. First Miss Mayfair, she act dat a-way, and
den Miss 'Collum she act dis a-way, an' dey bofe look like
dey'd swallowed cowcumbers and ice-cream. Lub nebber
affected dis chile dat bad. Yah! yah!

MAY. (*solil.*) But he shall not see that I suffer! I shall
laugh as merrily as if I had never known him, and flirt desperately with the next man I meet. He shall see that the
sun doesn't rise and set in him. Ah! Eddie, what have
you?

EDDIE. (*holding out note*) Yere's a lettah from Mistah Van
Ars'len. Bery 'tic'lar business, he said.

MAY. (*eagerly*) Thank you, Eddie!

EDDIE. Yo's puffectly welcome, Missy. (*He returns to
his seat by door.*)

MAY. (*walking away*) I wonder what he wants? (*She
reads*) "Meet him!" He's cool! Last night he said I
was "fickle," "heartless"—now he wants me to meet him!
Am I a plaything that he can throw aside and take up when
His Majesty pleases? I'll not gratify him! I'll show him
a woman has spunk. I wonder what he really does want
to see me about? Can he be in earnest? I wonder if I
hadn't better see him just this once, and tell him that this

must end it all ? Yes—I will ! O Ward, Ward! (*She returns to centre*) Here, Eddie, is a twenty-five cent piece for your trouble.

EDDIE. T'ank yo', Missy. (*Exit* MAY, *door.*)

EDDIE. Yah ! She done feel bettah, too ! 'Specs dey'll hab some mo' yum-yummin' dis arternoon. Mus' be berry 'tic'lar, too. Ki yi ! One dollah an' a half fo' dis business. I hopes dey takes to writin' notes all day long. Dere's mo' in it fo' dis chicken dan dis yere squeezin' in de dark. Yah ! yah ! yah ! (*Enter* DOLLY, *door, in walking costume.*)

DOLLY. Eddie, you haven't seen Mr. Pennington, have you ?

EDDIE. Yeth'm ; seed him roun' yer somewhere. Reckon he's done gone fo' a walk.

DOLLY. Oh ! Thank you, Eddie, (*She walks hastily to right and disappears.*)

EDDIE. Deh's one ob 'em gone. I reckon sugar and molasses'll be berry cheap pretty soon. Unk, unk ! I begins to feel like I would like to do some spahkin' myself. I wondah ef I could fin' dat yaller Chloe 'round dah in de laundry ? I'se gwine to see, ennyhow. (*Enter* MR. PENN., *door.*)

MR. PENN. (*carelessly*) Anybody been along lately, Eddie ?

EDDIE. (*shyly*) Yeth, sah ! Some one jest gone dat a-way. (*Jerking his thumb in the direction* DOLLY *has taken.*)

MR. PENN. If you see Mr. Van Artsdalen, tell him I shall expect to see him in about half an hour. He will understand. (*Exit in same direction as* DOLLY.)

EDDIE. Reckon I'll hab to go find Chloe ; my bosom's jes' a bustin' wid luv ! Yah ! yah ! yah ! (*Exit.*)

· (*Curtain.*)

SCENE II, ACT III.

SCENE.—*A lawn overlooking the sea. Rustic bench on left and some shrubbery scattered about.*

(*Enter* DOLLY, *hastily, from right, crosses over to bench and looks in every direction.*)

DOLLY. He is not here yet. Oh! what will he say? My heart fails me. Suppose I come here to listen only to recriminations from him, 'twill kill me! Oh!—how my poor heart is beating!—He is coming, I think. I *will* be calm. I shall be looking out to sea, and not know of his presence until he speaks. (*Enter* PENN. *from right.*)

MR. PENN. Ah! She is there! How like May is to Dolly in figure. O Dolly, Dolly! How I do miss her! I can put no heart into this flirtation. Yes, I will, too! I am not a school boy to be scared by a pair of laughing eyes. (*He crosses over to the silent figure of* DOLLY.)

MR. PENN. (*gayly*) Good afternoon!

DOLLY. (*starting and turning*) Oh! how you startled me!

MR. PENN. (*starting in turn*) Good heavens! You? (*Sotto voce*) The notes must have gotten changed. That black rascal, Eddie, has mixed things up!

DOLLY. (*frigidly*) You seem disappointed. Perhaps I had better save you the trouble of explaining why you asked me to meet you here by leaving. (*She arises and moves toward right.*)

MR. PENN. Dolly!!

DOLLY. Well?

MR. PENN. I—I—you—you—

DOLLY. You are not very brilliant to-day, Mr. Pennington.

MR. PENN. (*desperately*) I am a fool, Dolly!

DOLLY. "An honest confession is good for the soul."

MR. PENN. Have you no pity?

DOLLY. (*coldly*) For what?

MR. PENN. For me!

DOLLY. I am "heartless," "cold," "fickle," "jealous," "trifling"—such are your words of last evening. What else can you expect from such a wretch as I?

MR. PENN. (*appealingly*) You know I didn't mean them!

DOLLY. On the same principle, when you call me "darling," "sweet," and "pet," I presume you do not mean them, either.

MR. PENN. Dolly, how can you talk so? You know I love you!

DOLLY. I have heard you say that before, but last night stands between.

MR. PENN. (*desperately*) Have you no mercy for me?

DOLLY. You had none for me.

MR. PENN. How pitiless a woman can be! Forgive me for intruding upon you. I shall leave you without troubling you further. Farewell!! (*He turns and starts toward the right.*)

DOLLY. Harry!

MR. PENN. (*coldly*) Well? (*Halting.*)

DOLLY. Do you really mean what you say?

MR. PENN. Do you believe me capable of jesting about my love? (*Moving away.*)

DOLLY. (*appealingly*) Harry!!

MR. PENN. (*returning a step*) What is it?

DOLLY. (*holding her arms outstretched tenderly*) Harry!!!

MR. PENN. Darling!!! (*They throw themselves into each other's arms. Eloquent silence.*)

DOLLY. (*archly*) Are you sorry that you were a bad boy, dear?

MR. PENN. (*fondly*) Drefful!

DOLLY. Then you may tiss me—jus' once! (EDDIE *and* CHLOE *enter right at this stage of proceedings and behold the scene.*)

EDDIE. (*to* CHLOE) Dere! Dey's at it, Chloe! Laws a-mussy, obsarbe him!

MR. PENN (*kissing* DOLLY) There! There! There! There! There!

EDDIE (*to* CHLOE) Dat's de way de white folks does it, Chloe. Yah! Yah! Dere! Dere! Dere! Dere! Dere! (*Kisses* CHLOE *in mocking imitation of* MR. PENN. *The two colored individuals are screened from the view of the occupants of the pavilion by an evergreen bush, but in full view of audience.*)

DOLLY. (*sitting closer*) Isn't it nice to think our troubles are all over?

MR. PENN. Scrumptious! But say, dear—!

DOLLY. What is it, pet?

MR. PENN. I've a confession to make. (N. B.—EDDIE *and* CHLOE *are peeping with deep interest all the time from behind the bush. Of course plenty of funny and suggestive pantomime may be enacted by the two.*)

DOLLY. (*interestedly*) What is it? Something naughty?

MR. PENN. Dreadful!

DOLLY. Don't tell me then!

MR. PENN. I didn't write that note to you.

DOLLY. (*drawing away from him*) For whom then, pray ?

MR. PENN. (*desperately*) I wrote it to May McCollum.

DOLLY. (*bursting into tears*) O Harry! Harry! you have deceived me! Oh! oh! my heart is breaking!

EDDIE. (*to* CHLOE) Jimini crimini! Heah comes an April shower! Dat's no way to make lub!

MR. PENN. (*frenziedly*) Listen, dear, while I explain!

DOLLY. (*sobbing*) You can't explain! Oh! leave me! leave me! and go to your May!

MR. PENN. (*frantically*) You must listen to me! After last night Ward and I made a plan to get up a flirtation with May and you—I with May, he with you.

DOLLY. How shameful!

MR. PENN. Terrible! And we agreed to write a note to each of you, asking you to meet us here a half hour apart; then we were to pretend we didn't care a pin for our old loves, and we thought maybe our supposed indifference would bring all right again. But somehow or other the notes have been changed, and you have gotten May's and she probably has yours, and everything is mixed up.

DOLLY. To think you would stoop to such means! Do you regret that the notes were wrongly delivered?

MR. PENN. Darling! (*He folds her in his arms.*)

EDDIE. Dey's off again, an' de sun am shinin'! We ain' far behind. Yah! yah! (*He imitates* MR. PENN.)

DOLLY. (*listening and looking to right*) Oh! here comes May. Come, dear, we must leave the field to her. I do hope she and Mr. Van Artsdalen will be as successful in coming to an understanding as we have been. Come! (*They both leave the pavilion and disappear to left.*)

EDDIE. Anudder one, Chloe! (*he kisses her*) We's right up wid de band waggin ebery time! Oh! dere's Missy 'Collum! She am a lookin' for dat 'tic'lar business, too, dem notes spoke about. He aint come yit. Reckon we can sit down an' look at de lan'scape awhile, till de nex' lesson. (*He and* CHLOE *sit with their faces to the sea on a bench behind the evergreen. Enter* MAY *from right.*)

MAY (*solil.*) I do believe Dolly and Mr. Pennington have made up. I'm sure I saw him kiss her just now. And I— Oh! my heart! I am still out with Ward. Ah! why did we quarrel? It takes two to make a quarrel they say. Perhaps I was too hasty. Oh! if my life should be blighted by a few words. Suppose he is cold. Pshaw! I can be equally so. He must make the first advances. I shall play the *role* of indifference. He is coming. I'll be busily reading my novel. (*Seats herself and opens a paper novel. Enter* MR. VAN, *right.*)

MR. VAN. Ah! I can just see Penn and May in the distance. The plot is working. Dolly is awaiting me. I wonder what in the deuce I will say to her! Oh! why did I make a fool of myself last night? Suppose Penn makes such desperate love to my darling as to win her! By George, I'd shoot him! How intently Dolly is reading. She has on one of May's wraps this afternoon. Oh! if it were only my love how happy I would be! (*he approaches*) Busy reading, I see!

MAY. (*turning slowly around*) Oh! it's you, is it?

MR. VAN. (*starting, sotto voce*) Heavens! (*aloud*) Good —good—good afternoon!

MAY. (*coolly*) Good afternoon.

MR. VAN. You startled me! I thought you were Miss Mayfair.

MAY. (*bitingly*) Perhaps the thought was father to a wish.

MR. VAN. Heaven forbid!

MAY. You are suspiciously emphatic. To what am I indebted for this note from you after last night? Am I to listen to more insults?

MR. VAN. Insults! O May!

MAY. Your very look was an insult last evening.

MR. VAN. (*stiffly*) Perhaps my presence then is an insult to-day. I will bid you a very good afternoon.

MAY. (*stiffly*) Good afternoon, Mr. Van Artsdalen. (*She resumes her book.*)

EDDIE. (*peeping around the bush*) Chloe, de secon' lesson am a gwine to be pos'poned by de looks ob tings. Dere seems to be a chill in de atmosphere ober dah. He's jus' a puttin' fo' home, an' she hab turned her back on him. I don' unstan' dese yere white folks ways of lubbin no how. (*He and* CHLOE *both watch the developments with deep interest.*)

MR. VAN. (*going slowly to right*) I shall never cross your path again!

MAY. (*coldly*) You promise what I felt a delicacy in requesting. Thanks! (*reading*).

MR. VAN. (*sotto voce*) How beautiful she is when she is angry! But is she so utterly heartless as she pretends to be? (*aloud*) MAY!!

MAY. (*turning slowly*) Haven't you gone yet? Is there anything more you wish to say?

MR. VAN. Yes, one thing.

MAY. Go on!

MR. VAN. (*tenderly*) I love you, dear!

MAY. (*still coldly*) You say it beautifully! But you show very poor taste in loving a " frivolous coquette," and an " incorrigible flirt. Such are the expressions you were pleased to apply to me at the dance last evening.

MR. VAN. (*humbly*) I take them all back.

MAY. To fling them at me again the next time you lose your temper!

MR. VAN. You have no feeling!

MAY. There! You are beginning already :

MR. VAN. (*desperately*) May, you will drive me into a frenzy! Can you sit there, and be utterly indifferent to the slow torture I am enduring?

MAY. You forget the long hours of the night, just passed, in which I endured the torture of a sleepless memory!

MR. VAN. You are a stone! You cannot forget and forgive! I shall not ask again!! (*He rushes across to right.*)

EDDIE. Yah! yah! He goin' like he done fo'got somefin', Chloe, guess me an' you hab to give white folks some lessons, oursel's, yah! (*He kisses her.*)

MAY. (*springing up*) Ward! Ward! Come back, please!

MR. VAN. (*gloomily*) Farewell forever! (*Still striding away.*)

MAY. (*sotto voce, wildly*) Oh! what have I done? What have I done? I have killed his love! (*aloud*) Ward, my darling, come to me!!

MR. VAN. (*halting*) Are you jesting, or rehearsing for a melodrama?

MAY. (*bursting into tears, and dropping into seat and burying her face in her hands on the back of the railing*) Oh! oh! You are killing me!

EDDIE. Golly, she am a playin' her trump kiard now, ef dem teahs don' fetch him nothin' will. Yeth sah! didn't I tell you? He's gwine back fit to kill himself!

MR. VAN. (*in alarm returning*) May! my precious! Forgive me! forgive me! (*He drops on his knees before her, and puts his arms about her.*)

EDDIE. O Lor'! he's jes' puttin' on de style! jes' as dey does in de lub scenes at the teatre. Yah! yah! Chloe, 'specs I'll hab to practice dat ar' movement, too! (*He drops down on his knees beside* CHLOE, *and makes extravagant mockery of* MR. VAN.)

MAY. (*sobbing hysterically*) Wa—Wa—Ward, forgive me pl—pl—please for be—be—being so cruel!

MR. VAN. Forgive you, my own! It is you that must forgive me.

MAY. I do! I do!

MR. VAN. (*taking her hands down, and holding her face between his hands*) Well, then, pet, stop crying, and say you love me.

MAY. (*slowly*) I—love—you! (*Eloquent eclipse.*)

EDDIE. (*taking* CHLOE'S *face between his hands, too*) Chloe, dat's anudder new fangle. But we's right wid de times. Dehs nothing slow 'bout us, chile, sho's you's bo'n!

MAY. (*starting*) Dear, I hear voices! Who is coming?

MR. VAN. (*looking*) Botheration! Mr. Colfax and Miss Walling are coming right this way. Come let us stroll further. (*They both arise and walk to left.*)

MAY. (*smiling*) There is no rest for the wicked—or for lovers! (*Exeunt both left.*)

EDDIE. Dat's the end of dis lesson, Chloe. Don' see no 'provement, gal, ober de ole fashion way ob lub makin'. Guess we'll stick to de same ole styles. None ob dis yere pawin' de air, and droppin' on yo' knees, fo' me. I ain' a makin' a show of myself fo' no gal, yah! yah! yah! An' dere comes Mistah Colfax, and Missy Walling. Dat settles it! Deys as prim as two church steeples. No lub dere. Guess we'd better take a promenade on de beach, Chloe. (*Exeunt both right background.*) *Enter, right,* BELLE *and* MR. COLFAX, *with portfolios.*)

COLFAX. Ha! ha! "The wicked flee when no man pursueth."

BELLE. Ha! ha! ha! What a pity it was to disturb that *tete-a-tete!* It was so touching. Evidently everything is all right again.

COLFAX. And they have been putting into practice what we have been writing about.

BELLE. I wish we could make that last chapter as realistic as the scene we have witnessed.

COLFAX. I think you have done very well, indeed. (*They enter pavilion—sit down—and open MS. portfolios.*)

BELLE. (*taking up some pages*) No, it does not suit me. The hero and heroine make love like puppets. Just listen! (*She reads.*) "'Fairest love, I adore you!' said Ethelbert, taking her lily white hand in his. 'It is wrong to adore anything of earthly clay,' said Alicia, giving him a pale, timid smile. 'But you are my life! my all!' said he passionately throwing himself at her feet and pressing her fingers to his lips"—There! ha! ha! ha! that strikes me as being perfectly ridiculous! Doesn't it you?

COLFAX. It does sound rather machine made. Ha! I have it! We will act it out!

BELLE. (*laughing*) A brilliant idea ! Let's have the scene, please !

COLFAX. (*arising and reading*) " The moon was sailing aloft through the shredded clouds, and her pale rays fell upon the garden of the Count. By the side of the murmuring fountain, the noble Ethelbert, and the woman of his heart —the lovely Alicia—stood. From the wide open windows of the ball-room, the sweet strains of a Strauss waltz were pouring. Moved by the perfect beauty of the night, Ethelbert turned to her—"

BELLE. That will do for the scene. Now for the acting. Begin, please.

COLFAX. (*laughing*) Well, here's at it ! (*He stoops a little and looks down at* BELLE). " Alicia, I have been trying all the evening to tell you—that I love you !"

BELLE. (*drooping her head timidly*) " Love me ? Surely you cannot mean what you say ! I am but a simple country maiden, and you—you are a distinguished nobleman !"

COLFAX. (*taking her hand*) " Alicia, hear me ! I have loved you since the first day I met you ! Oh ! my love ! my love ! do not say ' no ' or I shall die !"

BELLE. (*looking up timidly*) " Die for me ? You are jesting. A man wins a woman's love not by dying, but by living for it."

COLFAX. (*bending lower*) " Then let me live for you, my darling. Will you not say ' yes ?' "

BELLE. (*drooping her head and speaking softly*) " Ye–es !"

COLFAX. " Then say : ' I love you, Ethelbert !' "

BELLE. (*with expression*) " Dearest Ethelbert, I love you !" (*She drops his hand and turns away with a sigh.*)

COLFAX. (*starting back and looking at her sotto voce*) How beautiful she looked then ! Has my heart been sleeping, that she has stolen into it without my knowing it ? (*aloud*) Belle, darling !

BELLE. (*starting in affright*) Alicia, you mean, Mr. Colfax !

COLFAX. (*seizing her hand*) No ! no ! no ! the comedy is ended, the jest has vanished, the scales have fallen from my eyes, and I know, my darling, that I love you—you ! (*drawing her to him*) Oh ! is there the slightest hope for me, Belle ?

BELLE. Why, have you been blind so long ?

COLFAX. You love me ?

BELLE. I do—my love !

COLFAX. (*putting his arms about her*) At last I know what love is ! This is my entrance fee, dear. (*Kissing her.*)

BELLE. To what, Lennox ?

COLFAX. To the primary department of the School of Love. I want to take the whole course with you as teacher.

BELLE. (*smiling*) You must learn rapidly.

COLFAX. Oh! I shall want my diploma in a year.

BELLE. Diploma?

COLFAX. Yes, dear—A Marriage Certificate!

BELLE. (*burying her face on his shoulder*) Oh!! (*While they are standing by the bench in this position* MR. PENNINGTON *and* DOLLY, *and* MR. VAN ARTSDALEN *and* MAY *approach slyly, with fingers to their lips, and surround them. At a signal they all say loudly—" AHEM!!"* BELLE *and* MR. COLFAX *start and spring apart.*)

BELLE. Oh!

COLFAX. Ah!

THE QUARTETTE. Yum! yum!

DOLLY. The Literary Partnership is complete!

MAY. There is no longer a silent partner in the firm! (*All come close, and the girls kiss* BELLE.)

BELLE. (*recovering herself*) I see two other firms are reestablished at the old stands.

MR. VAN. (*to* MR. COLFAX) Congratulations, old fellow!

MR. PENN. (*to* MR. COLFAX) Mine, too, old man!

COLFAX. (*proudly*) Thanks! May we never have even a lover's quarrel, and all be happy forevermore!

ALL. Amen!

MR. VAN. The campaign has been brief but thrilling.

MR. PENN. And has been brought to a happy conclusion with only three engagements.

COLFAX. We have met the enemy—

MR. VAN.
and ⎫ (*in chorus*) And we are theirs!
MR. PENN. ⎭

BELLE. Is it an unconditional surrender?

THE MEN. (*in chorus*) It is!!

TABLEAU.—*Each couple embraces and just as the curtain begins to descend,* EDDIE *and* CHLOE *appear in the background, witness the scene, and* EDDIE *exclaims:* " *Yah! Yah! Yah! dese yere white folks tinks deys got a monopoly on dis lub makin', but dey's mistaken, sho'! Chloe, we trabbels right along wid de people! Ki yi!*" (*He throws his arms about his sweetheart also, and kisses her with a resounding smack, as the curtain drops.*)

(*Curtain.*)

www.ingramcontent.com/pod-product-compliance
Lightning Source LLC
Chambersburg PA
CBHW061236260626
47172CB00003B/877